CAPTAIN DUCK

For Dad with love

Captain Duck
 www.harperchildrens.com

Library of Congress Cataloging-in-Publication Data
Alborough, Jez. Captain Duck / Jez Alborough. p. cm.
Summary: Duck causes trouble when he takes off in Goat's boat, carrying Frog and Sheep along with him.
ISBN 0-06-052123-6. [1. Boats and boating—Fiction. 2. Ducks—Fiction. 3. Animals—Fiction. 4. Stories in rhyme.] I. Title.
PZ8.3.A33 Cap 2003 [E]—dc21 2002068892 CIP AC

1 2 3 4 5 6 7 8 9 10 ❖ First U.S. edition, HarperCollins Publishers, Inc., 2003
Originally published in Great Britain by HarperCollins Publishers Ltd., 2002

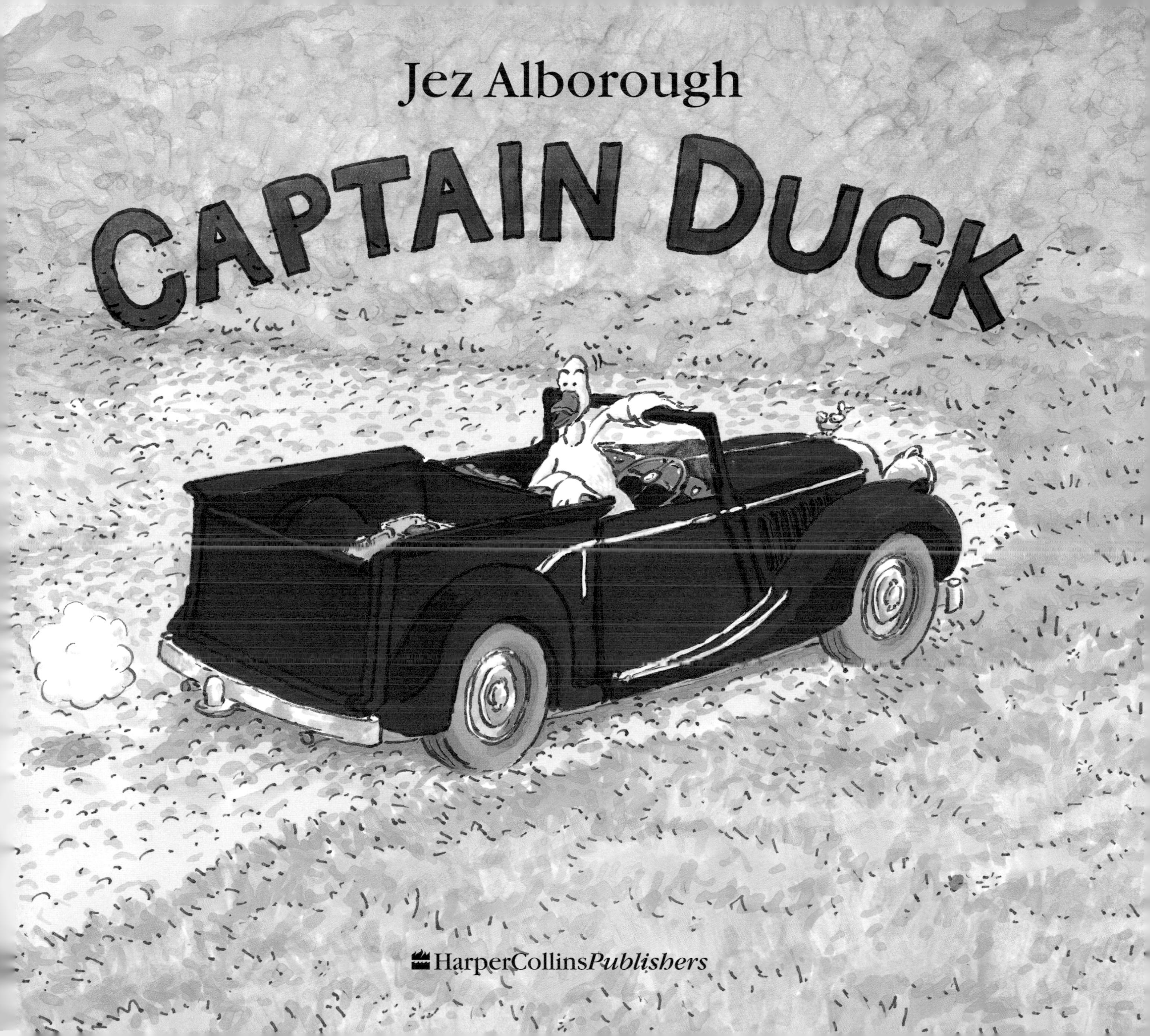
Jez Alborough
CAPTAIN DUCK
HarperCollinsPublishers

Pop, pop, coughs the spluttering truck.
"No more fuel left," quacks Duck.

"It's good I stopped
near my friend Goat—

he uses fuel
in his boat."

Duck *rap-tap-tap*s at Goat's back door,
waits awhile, then taps once more.

Still no answer,
so instead

he sneaks a peek
inside Goat's shed.

"Hooray!" cries Duck.
"A stroke of luck—

fuel for my
thirsty truck.

I'll only take a drop or two. . . .
Look, there's Frog! Where's he off to?"

He's off to take a trip on a boat.
"Hello!" calls Sheep. "Hop in!" says Goat.

"There's one last thing I need to bring. . . .
Now while I'm gone, don't pull that string."

They check the map
and pack the snack.

Then suddenly
they hear a quack.

“Ahoy there, sailors!” comes a cry.

“Is this a boating trip I spy?

If there are seas to be explored,

make way... CAPTAIN DUCK'S ON BOARD!

“Let’s get going!
What’s this thing?”

“No!” cries Frog.
“Don’t pull that string!”

The engine roars. Frog gives a shout.
“Oh, no!” screams Sheep. “Frog’s fallen out!”

"Grab that rope," says Duck. "I'll steer.
Throw it out when we get near.

Ready. . . steady. . . get set . . .THROW!
Catch!" yells Duck. "And here we go.

"I didn't know Frog could water-ski."

"No," bleats Sheep. "Neither did he.

Oh, please, Duck, please don't go too far.

Goat will wonder where we are.
I think you'd better stop it now. . . ."

"I can't," yells Duck. "I don't know how. Besides, we've

only just begun . . .

and Frog is having so much fun."

So Captain Duck steers the boat far away from poor old Goat,

who finds his can beside a truck.

"Aha!" he says. "That naughty Duck."

The little boat bobs on and on

until the riverbanks are gone.

Just then the engine
*pop-pop-pop*s

and with a final
cough it stops.

The stormy waves begin to swell.
Sheep says, "I don't feel too well."

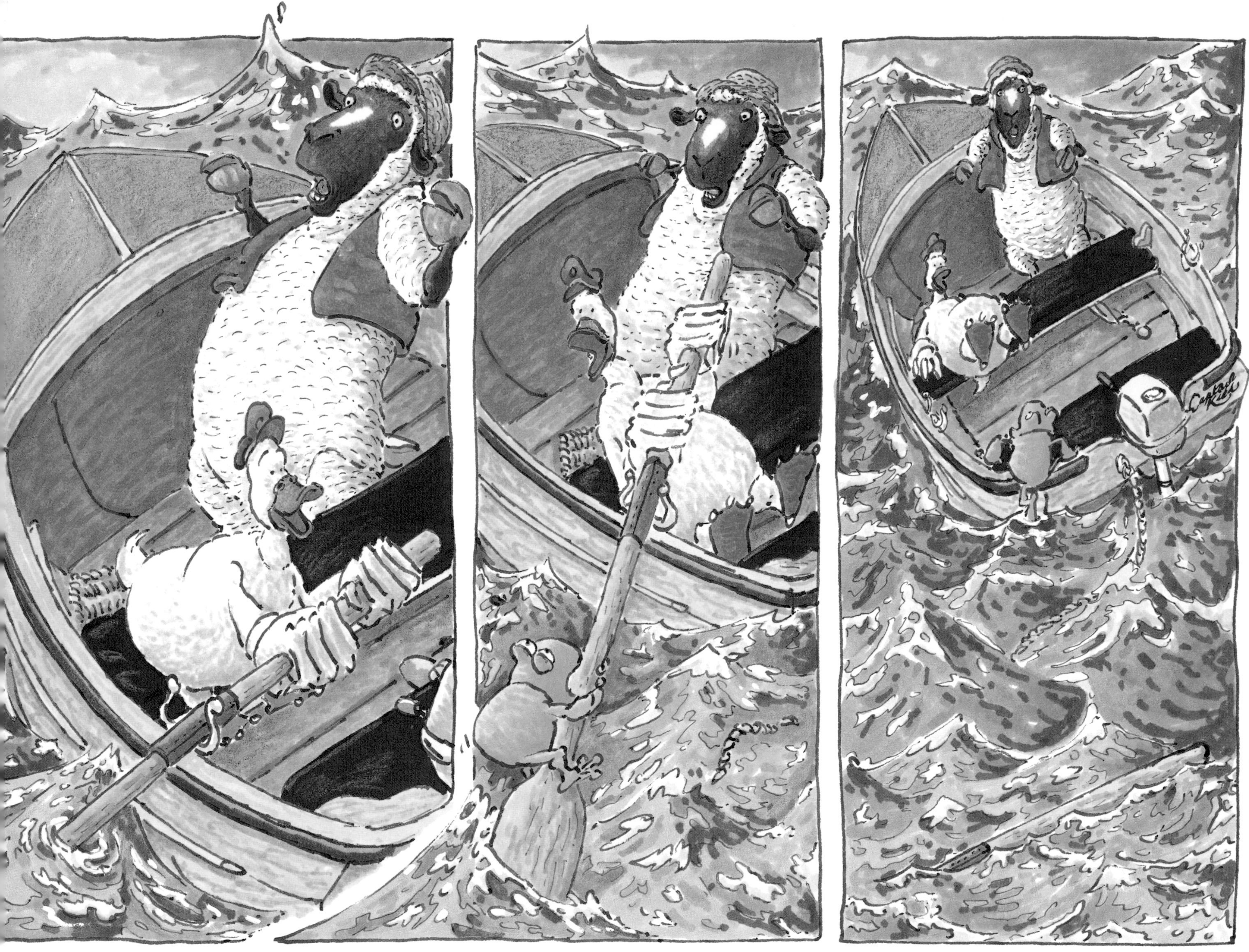

"Come on," says Duck,
"we'll row to shore."

"We can't,"
gasps Frog.

"There's just
one oar."

They huddle in the bobbing boat
and snuggle close to Sheep's warm coat.

And there upon the restless deep

three lost friends fall fast asleep.

Through the night,
hour by hour,

Goat keeps lookout
from his tower.

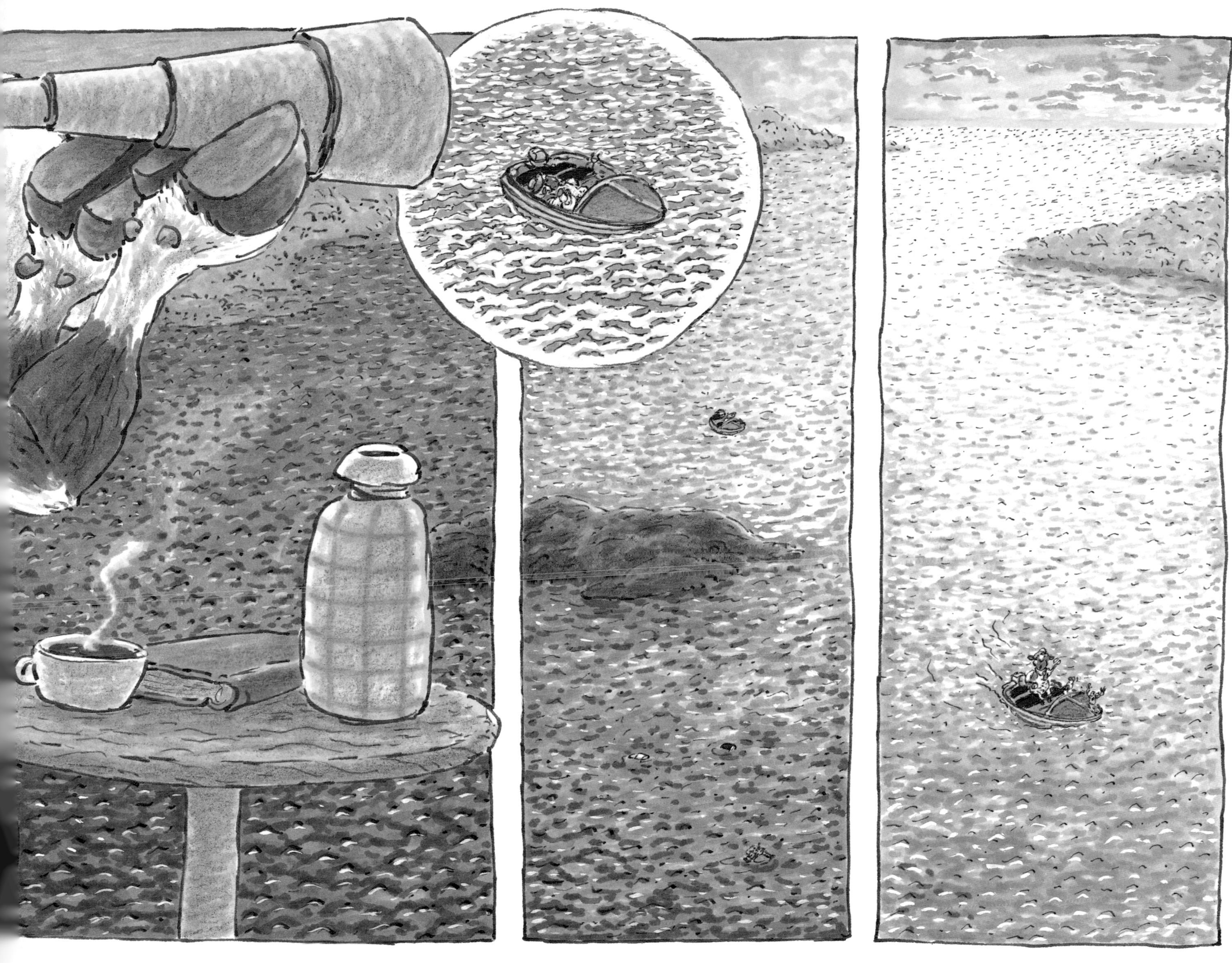

And then at dawn,
through bleary eyes, upon the tide his boat he spies.

Sheep calls out, "We're sorry, Goat.
We left you here . . . we broke your boat!"

"Broken?" says Goat as Duck tries to hide.
"Oh, no, it just needed fuel inside.

That’s why I went back for the can I keep spare.
I searched through my shed, but the can wasn’t there.”

“Wait!” says Frog. “Duck was holding a can!
It was just before our boat trip began.

So Duck took the fuel.” “That’s right,” says Goat.
“Now you know why there wasn’t enough in the boat.”

"Look! Duck's getting away!" Sheep cries.

"No, he's not!" gloats Goat with a glint in his eyes.

"He took the fuel,
that silly Duck,

but forgot to pour it into his truck!"

Captain Kidd